Morgan
The Clydesdale Pony

Written, Narrated & Music by Skip Martin

Illustrated by Gracie Green

Published by Gloryland Enterprises, L.LC.

www.jamesholmeslaw.com

Morgan The Clydesdale Pony is produced by the Law Office of James Holmes

ISBN: 978-1-7334711-9-0

e-book ISBN: 978-1-7334711-3-8

LCCN: 2019912938

Written, Narrated & Music:	Skip Martin
Illustrations:	Gracie Green
Editing:	Margaret Holmes, James Holmes, and Sandra Siler
Piano:	Sandra Siler
Design:	Jutta Medina

First Printing

Manufactured in the United States of America.

I dedicate this book to the wild-eyed next generation

of children & dreamers everywhere.

I am thankful to my grandparents for passing on the love of story telling

which gave me the tools to evolve into a storyteller.

"You can be anything, anything, anything...you can be anything...if you believe..."

ACKNOWLEDGMENTS:

Blessed and thankful for such an exceptional team in making my book a reality –

my business partner, Sandra Siler,

James Holmes, Margaret Holmes,

Gracie Green, Rachel Sherrill,

Kimberly Maxi Bond,

Sybille Duncan and Alex Blair.

I'm also grateful for the love and support of my family:

Sybille, my Mom Pearlyn, Lory, George, Steavin, Sennie, Primrose & Laila!

Hi, my name is Morgan.

And I'm a Clydesdale.

I led the firehouse stagecoach team

of Clydesdale horses for 11 years.

Most of my life, I had dreams of being in

the Kentucky Derby.

6

When I was just a pony, I saw

racehorses running in the Derby.

They were tall, beautiful and sleek!

They could run like the wind!

Every morning, I would eat my hay,

run around in my corral and tell my friends that

one day, I would win the Kentucky Derby.

Yeah, because...

"You can be anything, anything, anything...you can be anything...if you believe..."

Kool Aid the Barn Rat said,

"Shabba-dabba-doo-wop! – No way!"

Sasha the Cat purred,

"Mee-eow-How? Mee-eow-How?

—You so crazy!"

Millie the Cow said,

"You gotta moooooove real fast!

You moooooove too slow!"

Oscar the Barn Owl hooted,

"Who? Who? Who?
Who do you think you are?"

And Pokey the Pig

just grunted,

(grunt, grunt)

"Foolish,

(grunt grunt)

Foolish pony!"

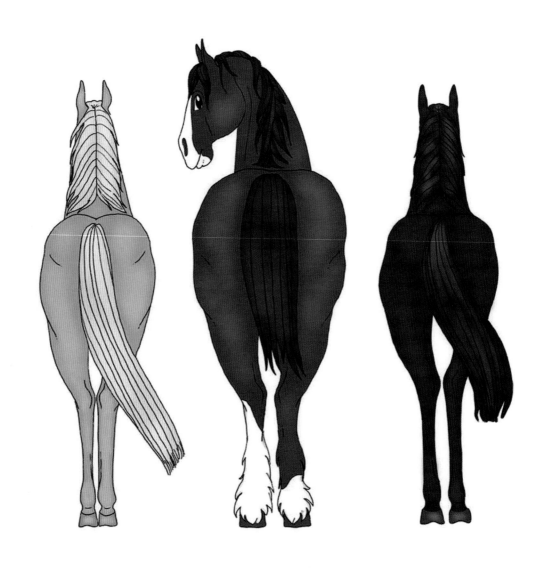

As I grew older, I got bigger, wider and stronger.

I was twice as wide as the race horses
and twice as strong.

But I was also twice as slow!

Still, I never gave up on my dream.

No, I didn't because...

One spring, horses from all over the world
came to run in the Kentucky Derby.

The most famous horse was Big Red.

Everyone knew he would win!

On race day, people filled the
grandstands in their finest clothes.

Kool Aid and Oscar put on their long-tailed
coats with brightly colored vests!

Sasha and Millie wore big feathered hats!

But Pokey just grunted,
"Loser, (grunt, grunt, grunt) loser
(grunt, grunt)!"

Big Red led the race on
a practice lap.

And suddenly, a huge rainstorm
swept over the track.

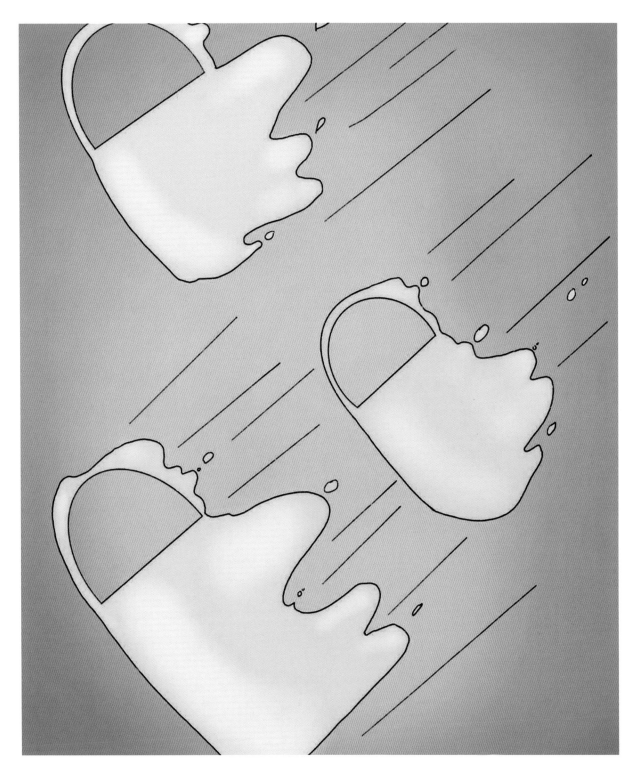

Lightning flashed, thunder crashed and rain fell like buckets.

The track turned into a muddy swamp!

On the last turn,

Big Red slipped in the mud

and crashed head over heels

in the muck!

Six more horses slipped and fell on top of him!

The crowd gasped, "Oh no!"

Big Red got to his feet, but something was wrong...

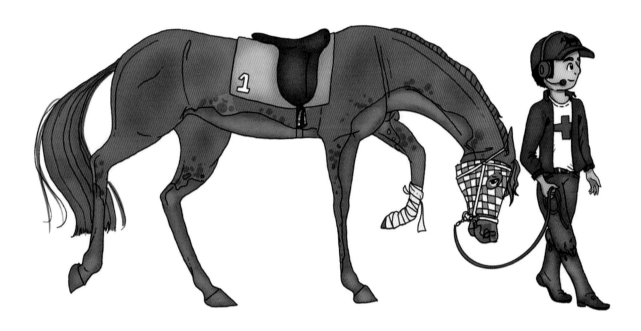

He limped back to the stables,

disappointed that he couldn't run in the Derby.

Still, the bugler played

the call to post—

bum ba ta, bum pa ta, bum bum bum bum!

My owner and Big Red's jockey looked at me.

I thought to myself, "Could this be the day
I've been waiting for my whole life?
Really?"

My owner said, "Morgan, I need you today.

Are you ready?"

30

And I said in a big horsey way,

"Yeahehehehe ha!"

Yeah, because...

The men dressed me in a blanket and a racing saddle.

I was looking good!

I trotted to the gates
and stood next to
the other race horses.

I could hear them breathing heavy
as my heart started just pounding in my chest!

32

RIIING!

"They're off in the Kentucky Derby!"
shouted the announcer.

My gate opened,
and I bolted out onto the track.

I ran as fast as I could.

All I could see was hooves and tails!

And through the second turn,
I fell even further behind.

On the backstretch, the other horses
began to slip and slide.

My big feet didn't
slip a bit!

And I was holding my ground!

When we got into the third turn,
the announcer raised his voice.

"And here they come down the
track in the backstretch!"

The crowd roared as I turned for home!

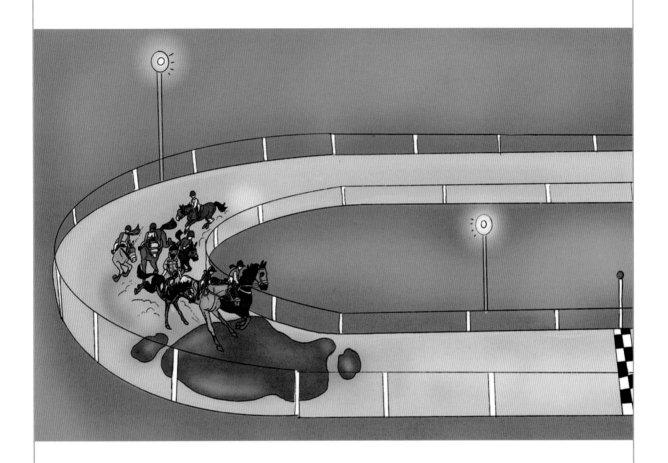

I saw race horses coming to that pond-sized
puddle where Big Red fell.

It looked like a big, glass table top
lying on the race track.

The lead horse plunged into that puddle, and
he slipped and fell, head over heels,
as the other horses fell on the top of him!

Just like what happened to Big Red!

My jockey said,
"Come on Morgan. Now's our chance!"
as he steered me to the right.

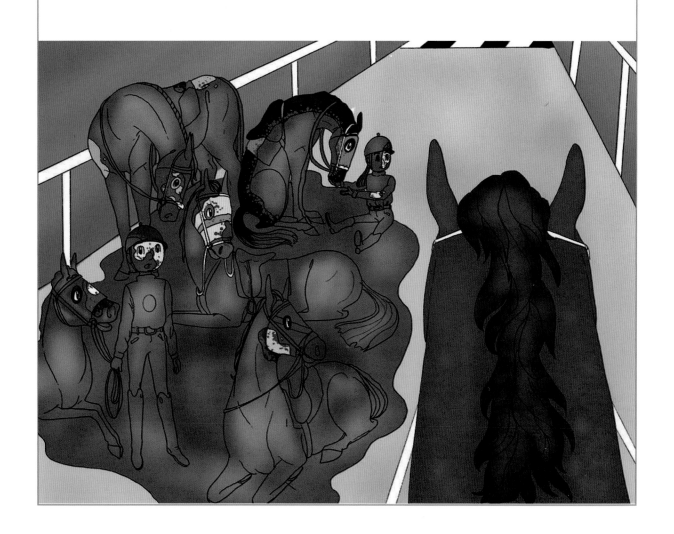

We ran around a pile of
muddy horses and jockeys.
They all looked like they were made of chocolate!

My jockey yelled, "Keep going, Morgan!
We're almost there!"

I saw Kool Aid the Rat and Millie the Cow
standing at the inside rail.

Millie shouted, "Come on, Morgan!
Mooooooove! Mooooooove! Come on!"

Kool Aid said, "Shabba Doo Wee! Now you can do it!"

I put my head down and galloped as fast as I could!

As I crossed the finish line in first place,
everyone cheered my name!
"Morgan, Morgan!"

"Yippee!" cried my jockey.

"You! Who!"
hooted Oscar the Owl.

"Mee-eow-Wow!
Mee-eow-Wow!"
purred Sasha the Cat.

And even Pokey the Pig cheered,

"(grunt grunt) First Place (grunt grunt) Winner!"

I pranced to the Winner's Circle.

And the stewards gave me a blanket of red roses,
and a trophy and a blue ribbon.

I had the biggest smile on my face
because my dream came true.

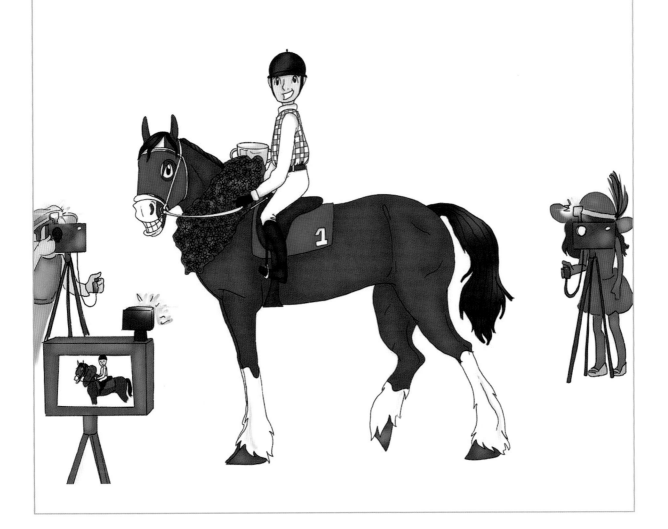

That was the happiest day of my life.

Because...

"You can be anything, anything, anything...you can be anything...if you believe..."

After that, I went back to the farm.

And I led the firehouse
stagecoach team for 11 years.

I ate my hay and trotted around my corral
like a thoroughbred race horse.

My friends clapped and cheered.

But today is the greatest day of my life.

Because, my son told me,
"Daddy, I want to be a racehorse."

And I said to him, "Son, you can be anything you want to be if you believe it in your heart."

"Even if you are JUST a Clydesdale pony."

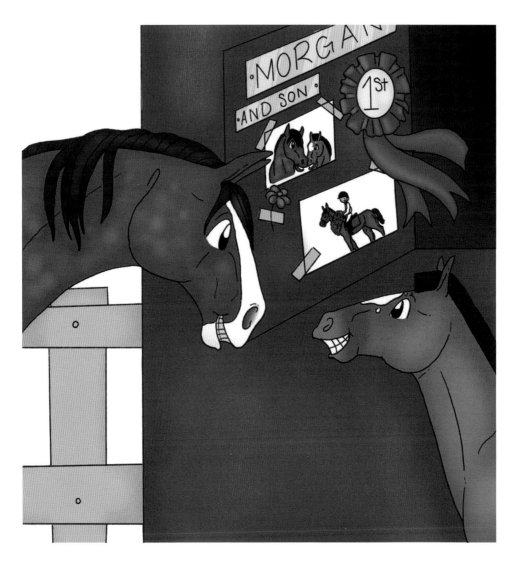

Yeah - Because...

My name is Gracie Green and I am 14 years old.

I was born in Georgia, but I have lived in Texas most of my life. San Antonio and Katy, Texas are home to me. I am home schooled and have been for 2 years now. I have two younger brothers, Noah who is 11, and Bowen who is 4. I also have a golden retriever named Duke. He is my little buddy and goes almost everywhere with me.

I have been drawing since I was old enough to hold a pencil. Although, I love drawing many things, horses have always been the stars of my sketchbook.

My slight obsession has grown as I have gotten older and horses have become a big part of my Life , always making the top of my Birthday Wish List. However, my wish to have a horse of my own hasn't come true yet. I have been blessed to take riding lessons and spend time with these wonderful creatures. I'm not giving up of that birthday wish just yet!

In my future I hope to become a part-time illustrator and an Equine Veterinarian. But my BIG dream is to own an equestrian center, where people can board their horses, ride, and have riding lessons. It will also be where my Equine Veterinary office will be. And of course I will always have my sketchbook nearby.

When it comes to my idols in life and the people I look up to, my parents, my Aunt Rachel, my Meemaw, and my Nana are definitely at the top of my list. I look up to them as artists and good people.

This was my first time ever illustrating a book. During this process I found out being an illustrator takes a lot of determination and a good mindset. I remember when first starting the illustration process, I sketched the characters and got a good feel of what they looked like and the way I would draw them. Then after that I turned my sketches into the final digital drawings.

The more detailed illustrations took the most determination and good mindset. Some taking up to 8 hours to complete! Trying to keep the characters looking consistent throughout the book was probably the most difficult part.

Now that the book is finished I am grateful for the difficulties. They are gained experiences and have helped me grow.

I would just like to thank my Uncle Jamey Holmes and Skip Martin for this opportunity, and the exposure for me as an artist. I would also like to thank my parents and Aunt Rachel for supporting and helping me through the whole illustration process. I couldn't be any more grateful for all of these new blessings in my life.

Morgan, The Clydesdale Pony's
exciting young illustrator

Gracie Green

Margaret and James Holmes

Margaret Holmes raised Jamey and five other sons in Buna, Texas. She is a proud member of the Red Hat Society and her bowling team. She published her first book, *Polly & The Polka Dotted House*, when she was 80 years old. Rachel Sherrill is her granddaughter. Gracie Green is her great-granddaughter. Jamey is a lawyer in Henderson, Texas. He is proud of his mom and his nieces.

Rachel Sherrill

Rachel Sherrill is Gracie's Aunt and Mentor. Rachel is a Potter and Silversmith in small town Maypearl, TX. Gracie and Rachel have always been very close and they have a special bond through their art. When she isn't creating, Rachel is doing her most important job which is being a wife and mother.

Sandra Siler

Sandra Siler is Skip's business partner and manager for USA events. Ms. Siler holds a Master's Degree of Art in Piano Performance from Southern Methodist University and was Head of Piano Instruction at Kilgore College in the city of Kilgore, Texas, for twenty-five years. Her love for music, performance, people and collaborating with others makes her the perfect complement for Skip's endeavors.

Follow Skip Martin:

WEBSITE
www.skipmartinmusic.com
FACEBOOK
www.facebook.com/skipmartinmusic
TWITTER
www.twitter.com/skipmartinmusic
INSTAGRAM
www.instagram.com/skipmartinmusic

For more information

on Skip Martin

please contact:

Gloryland Enterprises, LLC

Sandra Siler

sandra@glorylandenterprisesllc.com

BIOGRAPHY

Skip Martin is a Grammy Award winning artist, songwriter, producer and author, best known for his tenure as a lead singer and trumpeter for two legendary groups, Kool & the Gang and The Dazz Band.

His achievements include MOBO Outstanding Achievement Award, Platinum & Gold Record recipient, R&B Song of the Year, six consecutive Top 100 albums, two Top 100 singles, to name a few.

Mr. Martin has also received an Honorary Degree of Doctor in Music, several Certificates of Appreciation for his numerous tours to Iraq and Kuwait and is a Special Honorary Member of the United States Air Force Heritage of America Band. In addition, Skip is also Goodwill Ambassador to Kakegawa City and Okinawa, Japan. This is the very first time a resident of a foreign country has received this honor in Okinawa.

Skip's endeavors don't end with just music. He writes books, travels the world documented in his vlog #tripwithskip, loves to fish, hike and enjoys every aspect of nature.

His audio book 'Fables of a Paid Piper' is a collection of short stories chronicling life changing moments and experiences including meeting his hero Muhammad Ali.

But Skip's main passion is for people. You can find him helping kids follow their dreams, exploring their passions and creating new friendships. Skip lives to inspire with his story , undying love for the human race and, of course, his God-given musical talent.

Skip Martin

Photo Credit: Kouichi Teragishi